CHARLIE
and the Missing Music

Learning About God's Concern for the Lost

Mary Hollingsworth

as

Professor Scribbler

retells the Parable of the Lost Coin

Illustrated By
Peeler-Rose Productions

Brownlow

Brownlow Publishing Company, Inc.

DEDICATION

To
The Richland Hills
Family Singers
with love

A SPECIAL BOOK

For

_____

_____

From

_____

_____

_____

Date

Dear Parents and Teachers,

"Lost!" For a child, and even for adults, there is nothing more frightening than being lost — separated from those we love and who love us. And, nothing is more frustrating than losing something important to us. The process of searching for the lost item is tedious and nerve racking.

And, yet, don't we go on looking until we have found the missing item or until we are completely convinced that it simply cannot be found again? We don't give up hope easily. The more important the item is, the longer and harder we look for it.

Jesus told his disciples the story about a woman who lost something that was very special and important to her:

> *Suppose a woman has ten silver coins, but she loses one of them. She will light a lamp and clean the house. She will look carefully for the coin until she finds it. And when she finds it, she will call her friends and neighbors and say, "Be happy with me because I have found the coin that I lost!" In the same way, there is joy before the angels of God when one sinner changes his heart. (Luke 15:8-10, ICB)*

In our affluent society, losing one coin doesn't seem to be such a disaster. Scholars tell us, though, that this was a very special coin — one of ten that may have been her wedding gift from her husband. It held both financial and sentimental value for her. So, she looked desperately until she found it.

To a musician-composer, a musical composition is like a child to its creator. It holds both sentimental and, probably, financial importance to the composer. In this new *Adventure of Charlie Wandermouse*, Charlie somehow loses one of ten magnificent choruses he has composed for a very special concert. So, he and Professor Scribbler and the Cheddartown Singers turn the City of Musik upside down in search of the missing music.

In a simple way, this adventure will help your child or student learn these important lessons that Jesus was illustrating with the parable of the lost coin; (1) the state of being "lost" is tragic and hurtful, (2) we need to always be looking for the "lost" and (3) don't give up! What great spiritual implications there are for us and our children in this allegory.

Charlie and the Missing Music will give you an excellent opportunity to talk to your child about the importance of not becoming lost, about always looking for those who are lost and about being persistent until the lost is found.

It's off to the City of Musik now with Charlie and Professor Scribbler! So, pack your bags and climb aboard for an exciting adventure into the world of mice and music! And don't get lost on the way.

The Publisher

Hello. I'm a writer named Professor Scribbler. And this is my best friend, Charlie Wandermouse — world famous musician, traveler and explorer. This is one of my favorite stories about the time Charlie lost his greatest masterpiece and all the trouble it caused. It's a real adventure!

One bright, sunny day Charlie and I were relaxing on the banks of Flitterpond just outside Cheddartown. Charlie was stretched out in the hot sun taking a short snooze. And I was writing poetry in the cool shade of my favorite fern leaf.

Suddenly, Flora Flittermouse, who owns the mouse boardinghouse where Charlie and I live, came running toward us. She had a mouse-o-gram for Charlie. He sat up, rubbing his sleepy eyes, took the mouse-o-gram and ripped it open. Then Charlie's eyes grew very big, his whiskers started twitching, and a huge grin came on his face.

"What is it, Charlie?" I asked.

"It's an invitation for the Cheddartown Singers to perform in the world famous City of Musik. They want us to sing at the dedication of the magnificent new Opera House. What an honor!"

Flora, who was one of the singers, began running around with glee. "I've got to tell everyone the good news," she said. "Why the Cheddartown Singers are going to be famous."

The next few weeks were a furry flurry of preparations for us. We had to make travel arrangements, learn music, and pack our bags.

Meanwhile, Charlie shut himself up in the studio at the boardinghouse to write the final song for our performance. Charlie was a musical genius, and we all knew it. But when he let us hear the song for the first time, we cheered until the roof shook. There were ten beautiful songs, and the last one was a masterpiece. It made my fur stand on end. Why, I believe it was the best music Charlie had ever composed!

Finally, the day before our concert, we arrived in the City of Musik on Transmouse Airways. We checked into the Big Cheese Hotel. Charlie put the music for the final song into his coat pocket. Then we spent the rest of the day touring the famous city. With only one day to sightsee, we rushed from place to place on the high-speed Mousetram. We saw music museums, statues of famous musicians and we heard performances in the parks.

By the time Charlie and I got back to the hotel that night, we were both pooped. And our little paws hurt from so much walking. So, we went straight to bed.

The next morning Charlie slept in while I went down to breakfast in the Blue Cheese Cafe. When I came back, Charlie was up frantically searching the room.

"What's wrong, Charlie?" I asked.

"Scribbler, I can't find the final song to our program!" he said in a panic. "I know it's got to be here somewhere. We have to find it! The concert's tonight."

"Well, mousetraps and catfur! Don't panic, Charlie," I said. "We'll find it."

We furiously searched the entire room. In fact, we turned nearly everything upside down. No music! Now, even I was beginning to panic. Without the last song, our concert would be a flop. And Charlie's reputation as a world famous conductor would be ruined!

And, frankly, writing about a has-been mouse musician wouldn't help my writing career much either!

"I must have lost the music while we were all sightseeing yesterday," moaned Charlie. "What are we going to do? I can't possibly rewrite it before tonight. And that music could be anywhere in this huge city."

"I've got an idea!" I said. So, I called a quick meeting of the group in the hotel lobby and explained the problem. Then each group of singers took a section of the city to search for the missing music. With worried looks, they all scampered away.

Brownie and Millicent Mouse took one group to Strauss Park. The day before Charlie and I had gone there to listen to some lovely waltzes.

They looked under park benches, in trash cans, all around the statue and even in the flowerbeds. They peered into the bushes, under the picnic tables and even into the musicians' horns. But no music!

Monty Mouse and Giggles, she's the one with a crazy laugh, led another team. They scampered through every room of the art museum and looked behind every painting. They looked beneath sculptures, under the rugs and behind the doors. They looked upstairs and downstairs. They even peeked into the museum director's pockets just to be sure. No music.

Clicker Mouse is our photographer and Gobbler
. . . well, he eats more cheese than any other known
mouse. They led another team through the huge
Imperial Palace looking for the missing music.

They looked in the chandeliers, under the
gold goblets, behind the royal drapes and in the
King's chambers. They searched the bedrooms,
the balcony, the dining room and the Queen's
sitting room. Still, no music!

The Cheddartown Singers had searched everywhere in the city, but no music was found. It seemed that Charlie's precious creation was lost once and for all. Sadly, we all sat in the hotel lobby wondering what would happen.

Charlie, however, was a professional musician. He stood up and said bravely, "Listen everyone. We've come this far and we can't stop now. Go and get ready and look your best. Meet me backstage at the Opera House. We're going to make people in Cheddartown proud of us tonight, no matter what!"

The concert began on time, and the Cheddartown Singers had never sung so well before. All the important musicians from around the world were in the huge audience. And they were going wild.

We were half-way through the ninth song. Suddenly, Brownie's little son, Kirk, scampered across the stage and laid a piece of music on Charlie's music stand. Charlie wiped a giant tear from his big, brown eyes and winked at us. We knew little Kirk had found the missing music!

Without a pause, Charlie directed the final song. We squeaked our little hearts out. It was fantastic! Then, Charlie and the Singers received thundering applause and a standing ovation.

After the concert, Charlie gave a big party for all his friends from Cheddartown. "Be happy with me!" said Charlie. "My masterpiece was missing, but now it has been found." So, they had a big celebration.

After the party, we walked back to the hotel. On the way, Charlie said, "Scribbler, I was terribly upset when I thought I had lost that tenth song that I created. Do you think that's how a father feels when one of his children is lost?"

"I'm sure it is, Charlie," I said. "Even more so. And he probably gives a big party, just like you did, when that child is found, too."

"Now, that's a neat father," said Charlie.

And I had to agree. Maybe that's the way God feels when one of his children is lost and then found.